Dear Parents and Teachers,

In an easy-reader format, **My Readers** introduce classic stories to children who are learning to read. Although favorite characters and time-tested tales are the basis for **My Readers**, the books tell completely new stories and are freshly and beautifully illustrated.

My Readers are available in three levels:

1 **Level One** is for the emergent reader and features repetitive language and word clues in the illustrations.

Level Two is for more advanced readers who still need support saying and understanding some words. Stories are longer with word clues in the illustrations.

Level Three is for independent, fluent readers who enjoy working out occasional unfamiliar words. The stories are longer and divided into chapters.

Encourage children to select books based on interests, not reading levels. Read aloud with children, showing them how to use the illustrations for clues. With adult guidance and rereading, children will eventually read the desired book on their own.

Here are some ways you might want to use this book with children:

- Talk about the title and the cover illustrations. Encourage the child to use these to predict what the story is about.
- Discuss the interior illustrations and try to piece together a story based on the pictures. Does the child want to change or adjust his first prediction?
- After children reread a story, suggest they retell or act out a favorite part.

My Readers will not only help children become readers, they will serve as an introduction to some of the finest classic children's books available today.

—LAURA ROBB
Educator and Reading Consultant

For activities and reading tips, visit myreadersonline.com.

To Bixby, Van, Aurora, and Marigold

—M. H.

An Imprint of Macmillan Children's Publishing Group

Printed in China by Toppan Leefung Printing Ltd., Dongguan City, Guangdong Province.
For information, address Square Fish, 175 Fifth Avenue, New York, NY 10010.

Square Fish books may be purchased for business or promotional use. For information on bulk purchases, please contact the Macmillan Corporate and Premium Sales Department at (800) 221-7945 x5442 or by e-mail at specialmarkets@macmillan.com.

Library of Congress Cataloging-in-Publication Data Available

ISBN 978-1-250-01768-0 (hardcover)
1 3 5 7 9 10 8 6 4 2
ISBN 978-1-250-01769-7 (paperback)
1 3 5 7 9 10 8 6 4 2

Book design by Patrick Collins/Véronique Lefèvre Sweet
Square Fish logo designed by Filomena Tuosto

First Edition: 2013

myreadersonline.com
mackids.com

This is a Level 1 book

Lexile 100L

The Velveteen Rabbit Christmas

Maria S. Barbo ❧ *illustrated by* Michael Hague

inspired by
Margery Williams's *The Velveteen Rabbit*

Macmillan Children's Publishing Group
New York

It was Christmas Eve!
The Boy and Rabbit
helped to get ready.

The Boy put balls on the tree.
Rabbit put a star on top.

The Boy hung stockings.
Rabbit hung candy canes.

The Boy clapped.
Rabbit hopped.

They both sang.

"Folly, lolly, la! Ha! Ha! HA!"

Hip

hop

flop!

Oh, no!

Where did Rabbit go?

"Here he is!"

DING-DONG.
The doorbell rang!
"Who is there?"

It was the whole family!
They came for dinner.

The Boy put forks
on the table.
Rabbit set the spoons.

The Boy clapped.
Rabbit hopped.

They both sang.

"Folly, lolly, la! Ha! Ha! HA!"

The Boy took Rabbit's paw.

“Sit next to me,” he said.

It was hard to sit still.

The Boy tapped.
Rabbit hopped.

Oops!
Rabbit slipped.
Rabbit fell down
down
down!

Where did Rabbit go?

He was under the table!

Rabbit saw feet, feet,
and more feet.

Uh, oh!

Where did the feet go?

Rabbit heard a *tap*.
Rabbit heard a *clap*.
Who was there?

“Here I am!”

The Boy took Rabbit's paw.
"Look!" he said.
"It's snowing!"

The whole family sang.

"Folly, lolly, la! Ha! Ha! HA!"

What a great Christmas!